Bob
is a
Unicorn

By Michelle Nelson-Schmidt

W9-BYK-593

Kane Miller
A DIVISION OF EDC PUBLISHING

Dedicated to all the hopers,
the dreamers and the ones of us that
don't quite fit so neatly
into a category or definition.

Kane Miller, A Division of EDC Publishing

Text and illustrations copyright © Michelle Nelson-Schmidt 2013

All rights reserved.
For information contact:
Kane Miller, A Division of EDC Publishing
PO Box 470663
Tulsa, OK 74147-0663
www.kanemiller.com
www.edcpub.com
www.usbornebooksandmore.com

Library of Congress Control Number: 2012944941

Manufactured by Regent Publishing Services, Hong Kong
Printed June 2018 in ShenZhen, Guangdong, China

Hardcover ISBN: 978-1-61067-155-2
Paperback ISBN: 978-1-61067-189-7

Bob is not a unicorn.
Everyone can see that.
Everyone but Bob.

Whoa, Bob. What are you supposed to be?

I'm a unicorn, Marvin. Can't you tell?

No.

Well, I am.

Hey, Bob.

Hey, Stella.

What are you supposed to be?

You can't tell?

No.

Hey, Bob.

Hey, Ted.

What's that thing?

It's my horn. I'm a unicorn. See?

No, not really.

Margo, you can tell what I am, right?

Besides silly?

George, I don't suppose you—

Bob, don't you have more important
things to do?

I'm being a unicorn today.

It looks like you're wasting time
to me.

Henry, look at me. Guess what I am.

Bob, I've been up since the crack of dawn.

Sorry, Henry.

Hi, Francis. Can you guess what I am?

I'm too old to play games, Bob.
Why don't you just tell me what you are.
I have things to do.

Never mind.

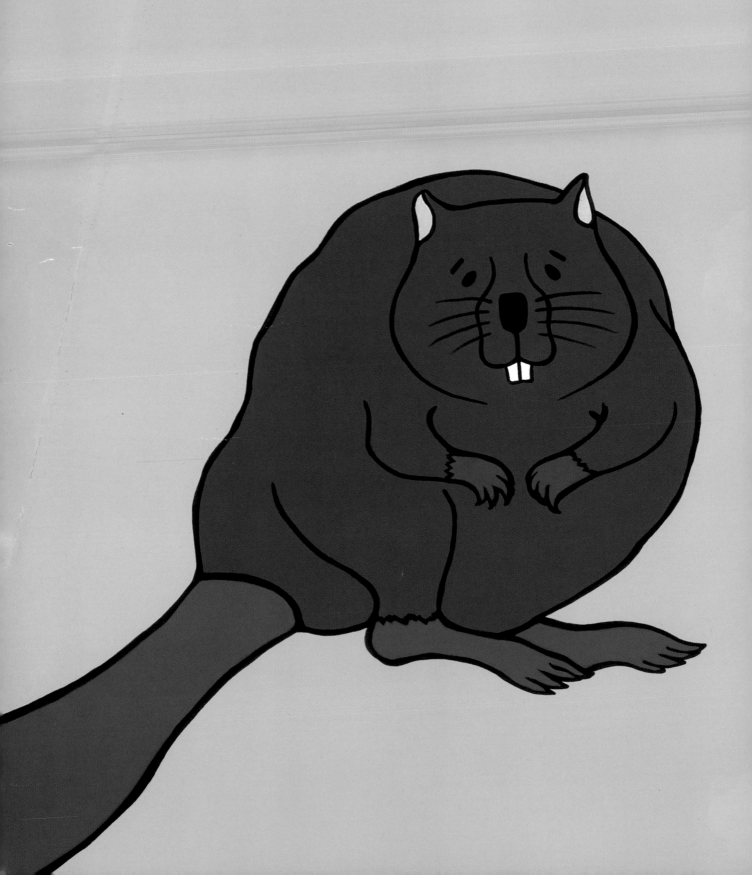

Hi, Larry. What are you doing?

Working, Bob. I'm working.
What is that? What are you up to?

I'm playing. It's—

I'm busy, Bob.

Bye, Larry.

Oh well.

Oh!

Look at you.
You are the best unicorn
I've ever seen.
What a beautiful horn.
And just look at your
mane. And the sparkles.

Let's play, Bob.

Yes, please.

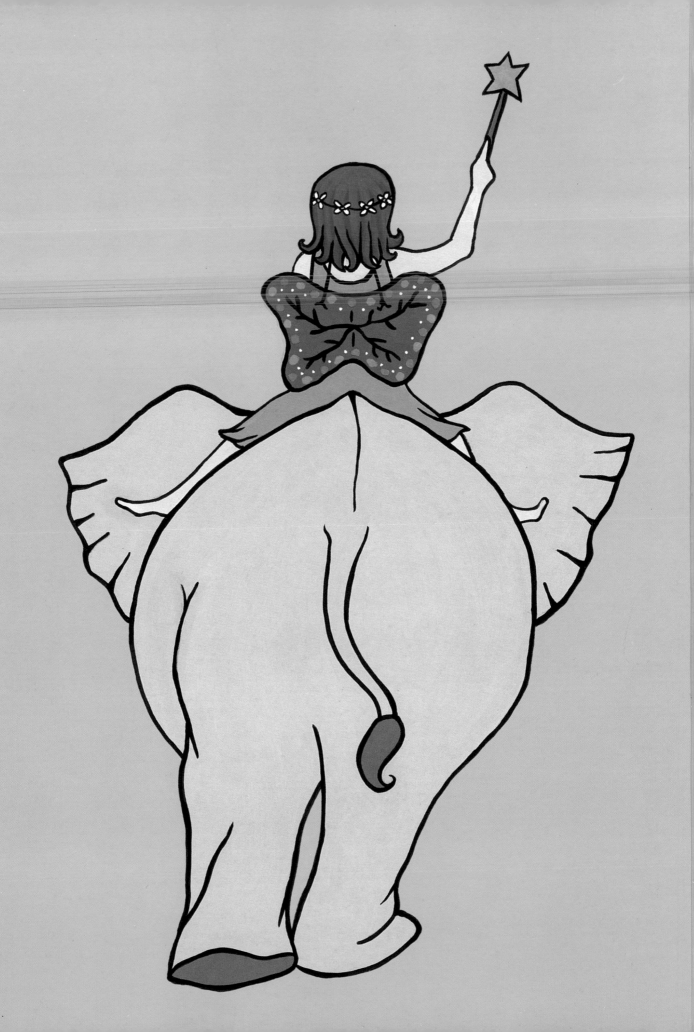